For Ellis and Harriet, heart of hearts
—J. S.

Library of Congress Cataloging-in-Publication Data. Sheppard, Jeff. Splash, splash / by Jeff Sheppard ; illustrated by Dennis Panek. — 1st ed.   p.   cm.
Summary: All kinds of animals, from a bee to a frog, fall into the water, making their own distinctive noises as they get wet. ISBN 0-02-782455-1   [1. Animal sounds—Fiction. 2. Animals—Fiction.   3. Stories in rhyme.] I. Panek, Dennis, ill.   II. Title. PZ8.3.S5524Sp 1994   [E]—dc20   92-26163

Splash, Splash

by Jeff Sheppard
illustrated by Dennis Panek

Macmillan Publishing Company   New York
Maxwell Macmillan Canada   Toronto
Maxwell Macmillan International   New York   Oxford   Singapore   Sydney

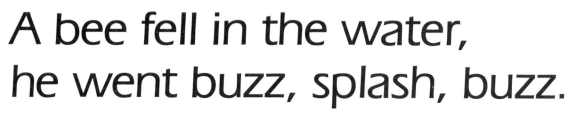

A bee fell in the water,
he went buzz, splash, buzz.

When a bee falls in the water,
that's what a bee does.

Bee says:
buzz, splash,

buzz, splash,

buzz.

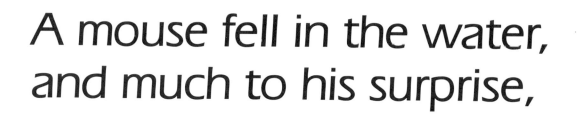

A mouse fell in the water,
and much to his surprise,

he got water in his ears,
he got water in his eyes.

Mouse says:
squeak, splash,

squeak, splash,

squeak.

A pig fell in the water
as he dreamed of eating cake.

He was about to have a bite,
when he landed in the lake.

Pig says: oink, splash,

oink, splash,

oink.

A dog fell in the water.
You know what he did then?

He liked it *sooooo* much that he fell in again!

Dog says:

ruff, splash,

ruff, splash,

ruff.

A cow fell in the water.
She looked a little grim.

Cows like to wade,
but cows don't like to swim.

Cow says:

moo, splash,

moo, splash,

moo.

A duck fell in the water, and ducks understand

paddling in the water
beats waddling on the land.

Duck says:
quack, splash,

quack, splash,

quack.

A cat fell in the water.
She wasn't pleased at all.

When cats fall in the water,
they look very, very small.

Cat says:
meow, splash,

meow, splash,

meow.

A frog fell in the water,

with his flappy, froggy feet.

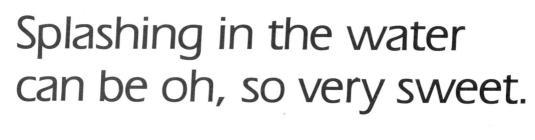

Splashing in the water
can be oh, so very sweet.

Frog says:
ribbit, splash,

ribbit, splash,

ribbit.

Diving and swimming,
wading and playing,

see if you can hear
what the animals are saying.